How to Analyze the Works of

STEPHENIE MEYER

by Marcela Kostihova

ABDO
Publishing Company

Essential Critiques

How to Analyze the Works of

STEPHENIE MEYER

by Marcela Kostihova

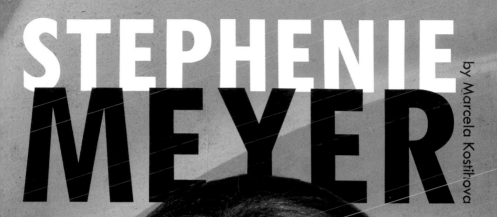

Content Consultant: Benjamin J. Robertson, instructor,
Department of English, University of Colorado at Boulder

Credits

Published by ABDO Publishing Company, 8000 West 78th Street, Edina, Minnesota 55439. Copyright © 2012 by Abdo Consulting Group, Inc. International copyrights reserved in all countries. No part of this book may be reproduced in any form without written permission from the publisher. The Essential Library™ is a trademark and logo of ABDO Publishing Company.

Printed in the United States of America,
North Mankato, Minnesota
062011
092011

 THIS BOOK CONTAINS AT LEAST 10% RECYCLED MATERIALS.

Editor: Amy Van Zee
Copy Editor: Sarah Beckman
Interior Design and Production: Marie Tupy
Cover Design: Marie Tupy

Library of Congress Cataloging-in-Publication Data
Kostihova, Marcela, 1974-
  How to analyze the works of Stephenie Meyer / by Marcela Kostihova.
    p. cm. -- (Essential critiques)
  Includes bibliographical references and index.
  ISBN 978-1-61783-094-5
1. Meyer, Stephenie, 1973---Criticism and interpretation. 2. Meyer, Stephenie,
1973- Twilight saga series. 3. Young adult fiction, American--History and criticism.
I. Title.
  PS3613.E979Z74 2011
  813'.6--dc22

                              2011007390

Table of Contents

Chapter

1

Introduction to Critiques

What Is Critical Theory?

What do you usually do when you read a book?
You probably absorb the specific language style of
the book. You learn about the characters as they are
developed through thoughts, dialogue, and other
interactions. You may like or dislike a character
more than others. You might be drawn in by the plot
of the book, eager to find out what happens at the
end. Yet these are only a few of many possible ways
of understanding and appreciating a book. What
if you are interested in delving more deeply? You
might want to learn more about the author and how
his or her personal background is reflected in the
book. Or you might want to examine what the book
says about society—how it depicts the roles of

women and minorities, for example. If so, you have
entered the realm of critical theory.

Critical theory helps you learn how various
works of art, literature, music, theater, film, and
other endeavors either support or challenge the way
society behaves. Critical theory is the evaluation
and interpretation of a work using different
philosophies, or schools of thought. Critical theory
can be used to understand all types of cultural
productions.

There are many different critical theories. If you
are analyzing literature, each theory asks you to
look at the work from a different perspective. Some
theories address social issues, while others focus on
the writer's life or the time period in which the book

was written or set. For example, the critical theory that asks how an author's life affected the work is called biographical criticism. Other common schools of criticism include historical criticism, feminist criticism, psychological criticism, and New Criticism, which examines a work solely within the context of the work itself.

What Is the Purpose of Critical Theory?

Critical theory can open your mind to new ways of thinking. It can help you evaluate a book from a new perspective, directing your attention to issues and messages you may not otherwise recognize in a work. For example, applying feminist criticism to a book may make you aware of female stereotypes perpetuated in the work. Applying a critical theory to a book helps you learn about the person who created it or the society that enjoyed it. You can also explore how the work is perceived by current cultures.

How Do You Apply Critical Theory?

You conduct a critique when you use a critical theory to examine and question a work. The theory you choose is a lens through which you can view the work, or a springboard for asking questions about the work. Applying a critical theory helps you think critically about the work. You are free to question the work and make an assertion about it. If you choose to examine a book using biographical theory, for example, you want to know how the author's personal background or education inspired or shaped the work. You could explore why the author was drawn to the story. For instance, are there any parallels between a particular character's life and the author's life?

Forming a Thesis

Ask your question and find answers in the work or other related materials. Then you can create a thesis. The thesis is the key point in your critique. It is your argument about the work based on the tenets, or beliefs, of the theory you are using. For example, if you are using biographical theory to ask how the author's life inspired the work, your thesis could be worded as follows: Writer Teng Xiong, raised in refugee camps

> **How to Make a Thesis Statement**
>
> In a critique, a thesis statement typically appears at the end of the introductory paragraph. It is usually only one sentence long and states the author's main idea.

in Southeast Asia, drew upon her experiences to write the novel *No Home for Me*.

Providing Evidence

Once you have formed a thesis, you must provide evidence to support it. Evidence might take the form of examples and quotations from the work itself—such as dialogue from a character. Articles about the book or personal interviews with the author might also support your ideas. You may wish to address what other critics have written about the work. Quotes from these individuals may help support your claim. If you find any quotes or examples that contradict your thesis, you will need to create an argument against them. For instance: Many critics have pointed to the protagonist of *No Home for Me* as a powerless victim of circumstances. However, in the chapter "My Destiny," she is clearly depicted as someone who seeks to shape her own future.

How to Support
a Thesis Statement

A critique should include several arguments. Arguments support a thesis claim. An argument is one or two sentences long and is supported by evidence from the work being discussed.

Organize the arguments into paragraphs. These paragraphs make up the body of the critique.

In This Book

In this book, you will read summaries of famous books by writer Stephenie Meyer, each followed by a critique. Each critique will use one theory and apply it to one work. Critical thinking sections will give you a chance to consider other theses and questions about the work. Did you agree with the author's application of the theory? What other questions are raised by the thesis and its arguments? You can also find out what other critics think about each particular book. Then, in the You Critique It section in the final pages of this book, you will have an opportunity to create your own critique.

Look for the Guides

Throughout the chapters that analyze the works, thesis statements have been highlighted. The box next to the thesis helps explain what questions are being raised about the work. Supporting arguments have been underlined. The boxes next to the arguments help explain how these points support the thesis. Look for these guides throughout each critique.

Author Stephenie Meyer

Chapter

2

A Closer Look at Stephenie Meyer

Stephenie Morgan (later Meyer) was born in Hartford, Connecticut, on Christmas Eve of 1973 to Stephen and Candy Morgan. In 1978, the Morgan family relocated to the Phoenix area in Arizona, where Stephenie's father found a job as a financial planner. It was in Arizona that Stephenie spent the rest of her childhood and young adulthood.

Mormon Upbringing

According to interviews, Stephenie's upbringing in the large Morgan family, in which she was the second of six children, was strict and firmly grounded in the beliefs of the Church of Jesus Christ of Latter-day Saints, also called the Mormon Church. After she graduated from high school in Scottsdale, Arizona, in 1992, Stephenie relocated to Utah.

There, she attended Brigham Young University, which is affiliated with the Church of Jesus Christ of Latter-day Saints. Stephenie has professed that her favorite book is the Book of Mormon. Her bachelor's degree, awarded in 1997, was in English. After graduation, she soon married her college boyfriend, Christian "Pancho" Meyer, taking his last name. Stephenie relinquished her public duties—except her ongoing service to her church—to be a homemaker.

The Idea for *Twilight* and Rise to Fame

By her own account, published on her official Web site and corroborated through numerous early interviews, Meyer's affair with the *Twilight* characters began in a vivid dream she had on June 2, 2003. In that dream, she saw two people in a beautiful meadow. These two were engaged in an intense conversation. According to Meyer's own recollection: "One of these people was just your average girl. The other person was fantastically beautiful, sparkly, and a vampire. They were discussing the difficulties inherent in the facts that A) they were falling in love with each other while B) the vampire was particularly attracted to the scent of her blood, and was having a difficult time restraining himself from killing her immediately."[1]

When Meyer woke up, she tried to capture and develop that dream, which became the seed of *Twilight*. Published in fall 2005, *Twilight* brought an unbelievable $750,000 in advanced pay from Little, Brown and Company and shortly catapulted Meyer to the *New York Times* best-seller list. By 2008, millions of fans were hooked on the novels *New Moon* (2006) and *Eclipse* (2007). Fans were impatiently waiting to purchase the last installment, *Breaking Dawn*, at midnight release parties. The series of four novels, collectively called The Twilight Saga, broke records in sales and landed on best-selling lists. Additionally, fans were swooning over Robert Pattinson's portrayal of Edward Cullen in the movie adaptations. Meyer appeared on *Time* magazine's list of the 100 most influential people in 2008 and the *Forbes* list of most powerful celebrities in 2009 and 2010.

Praise and Criticism

Meyer, who was in her thirties, skyrocketed from anonymity to notoriety. As the mother of three young children, Meyer's pursuits prior to

Twilight were decidedly domestic. Besides her writing training at Brigham Young, Meyer seems to have written little—and published nothing—prior to *Twilight*, prompting profilers in *Time* magazine and other news sources to label her the "Mormon Housewife turned novelist."[2] In this context, *Twilight* was an unexpected, fresh newcomer to the literary scene. The Twilight Saga has sold more than 115 million copies worldwide, suggesting that Meyer's writing struck a powerful chord with a generation of young readers. Although the series falls into the young-adult literature category, readers of all ages have enjoyed the books.

Simultaneously to the success of the series, her work engendered much lambasting and lampooning for its reported simplicity and immediately spawned several prominent parodies, including Stephen Jenner's *TwiLite: A Parody* (2009) and The Harvard Lampoon's *nightlight: a parody* (2009). Professional reviewers have similarly disagreed on the merit of Meyer's works. Yet, the response to her work is so tremendous that thousands of people show up to her book signings and enthusiastic fans dress up like her characters.

Meyer greets
fans at the
premiere of the
New Moon film
in 2009.

According to Meyer, the art on the *Twilight* cover represents Bella's choosing of the forbidden fruit.

3

An Overview of *Twilight*

The story begins when 17-year-old Bella Swan decides to move from sunny Arizona to rainy Forks, Washington, to live with her dad, Charlie, after her mother's remarriage. Initially, Bella is ambivalent about her decision: she does not like Forks's weather or its small-town high school. Nevertheless, she quickly becomes engrossed in her new life, thanks to the presence of a mysterious classmate, Edward Cullen, whom she finds exceedingly attractive. Startled by his apparent hostility, Bella spends considerable time thinking about him. Edward improbably saves her life by stopping a skidding van with his bare hands. Despite warning her that he is not good friend material, he begins to spend time with her at school and offers to give her a ride to Seattle for a planned shopping trip.

Secret Discovered

Bella cannot make sense of Edward's unorthodox behavior, irresistible looks, impressive intellect, abnormal physical strength, and uncanny ability to know what other people think. She receives unexpected help from her friend Jacob Black. Jacob tells her a legend of his Native American Quileute tribe, which suggests that Edward and his family (Carlisle, Esme, Rosalie, Emmett, Alice, and Jasper) might be vampires. At first, Bella doubts this suggestion. However, when Bella considers what she knows of Edward, she knows that the legend must be true and that she does not care.

When she confronts him, Edward admits he is a vampire and explains his coven's lifestyle. The group lives as vegetarians, surviving on the blood of animals instead of humans. The vampires are also immortal and possess special powers. These include Edward's mind-reading ability—an ability that he can exercise on anyone except Bella—and Alice's power to foresee the future. In addition to these revelations, Edward confesses an insatiable thirst for Bella's blood. He again warns her to stay away, but he shares that he is unable to keep away

from her. Instead of being afraid, Bella declares her eagerness to be with him even if that leads to her death. They begin to spend time together at school, and Edward proposes that they hike in the forest.

The day spent in a sunny meadow proves to be a turning point in their budding relationship. Bella realizes that vampire skin sparkles in the sun — the reason the Cullens live in rainy Forks — and Edward learns that his self-control is greater than his thirst. They discuss their love for each other and begin spending nights together as well, though they refrain from having sex (despite Bella's wishes to

The real city of Forks, Washington, has received many visitors from fans of The Twilight Saga.

the contrary) to not endanger Bella's life. Edward admits that he had been sneaking into Bella's house and bedroom for the past several months to observe her activities and her sleep patterns, but Bella is not alarmed. Edward introduces Bella to his coven, and he is formally introduced to Charlie as Bella's boyfriend.

A Fight to the Death

Their relationship is challenged by the unexpected arrival of a small coven of transient "traditional," nonvegetarian vampires: James, Victoria, and Laurent. Once James catches Bella's scent and realizes her importance to the Cullens, he sets out to destroy her. Alice and Jasper take Bella to hide in sunny Phoenix. The rest of the Cullens pursue James and Victoria, but the two evade them and James eventually follows Bella south.

There, James leads Bella to believe that he had captured her mother and persuades Bella to meet him. Bella sneaks away from her protectors to meet James, only to find that the kidnapping was a ruse and that her own impending death is intended to send a symbolic message to the Cullens. Edward, Carlisle, Emmett, Jasper, and Alice arrive in time to save Bella's life and destroy James.

Bella sustains a venomous vampire bite from James that, if untreated, will bring about her own transformation into a vampire. This presents Edward with a dilemma. He can let the transformation take its course, which would allow Bella to end her human life and join him in immortality as a vampire. Or, he can save Bella's life by sucking out the venom, a feat made difficult by his desire to drink her blood in its entirety. Edward decides to help Bella remain human.

Once Bella recovers, she requests to be turned into a vampire to spend eternity with Edward. He refuses, explaining his unwavering commitment to preserving her human experiences.

Twilight closes with Bella and Edward attending their high school prom—an occasion she hoped to miss altogether.

In the world of *Twilight*, the vampires are faster, stronger, and more beautiful than the humans around them.

How to Apply Structuralism to *Twilight*

No.2

What Is Structuralism?

Structuralism assumes that nothing can be understood in isolation but only as part of larger contexts. As a primary example, humans communicate through language, a collectively agreed upon structure of signs that label the world. This structure both enables and limits the understanding of this world: words help understand what is seen, but it is impossible to label—or fully understand—things or concepts for which there are no words.

Similarly, structuralism believes that human understanding functions relationally: a concept is only understood as it relates to other known concepts. The concept *medium*, for example, only makes sense in relation to its immediate structure, either in terms of size (and the concepts of *small* and *large*), cooking (in comparison to *rare* and *well done*), art (as applied to *watercolors* or *collage*), or the occult (as a form of communication with the supernatural).

As a critical approach, structuralism investigates texts in a variety of contexts, beginning with—but not limited to—structures offered by the texts themselves. According to author Lois Tyson, "Structuralism sees itself as a human science whose effort is to understand, in a systematic way, the fundamental structures that underlie all human experience."[1] Structuralists seek to find what underlying structures drive human behavior.

Applying Structuralism to *Twilight*

Twilight invites a structuralist interpretation in offering two explicit frameworks, each with its own set of norms. These are the competing worlds in the novel: the human world and the vampire world. In these two worlds, underlying principles related to economics and class structure reveal themselves in alarming ways. Taking into account the vampires' irresistible qualities, it is not difficult to determine that their world is represented as far more compelling than the mundane world of the perpetually stumbling, awkward, pitiable human beings. The novel suggests that this superiority entitles them to control humans. Considering this realization, what in the comparison of the two worlds determines the vampires' superiority? In *Twilight*, the vampires' superiority is defined explicitly in terms of social class, specifically through a traditional understanding of aristocracy. Through this comparison of the two worlds, the novel suggests an underlying economic principle: that those with more resources can and should control those who lack them.

    Twilight's humans are weak, breakable, irrational, inconsistent, boring, and generally pitiful. As the most relevant representative of humanity, Bella seems average at best. She has no

Thesis Statement

The thesis statement in this critique is: "In *Twilight*, the vampires' superiority is defined explicitly in terms of social class, specifically through a traditional understanding of aristocracy. Through this comparison of the two worlds, the novel suggests an underlying economic principle: that those with more resources can and should control those who lack them." The thesis answers the questions: What makes vampires seem so superior to humans? Why does it matter?

Argument One

The author has started to support the thesis. The first point is: "*Twilight*'s humans are weak, breakable, irrational, inconsistent, boring, and generally pitiful." She has started to show how the novel sets up humans as less interesting and less deserving.

interests, passions, or hobbies. She goes through life performing what is expected of her, and she generally lacks distinguishing characteristics—with the exception of her clumsiness. She defines herself through what she does not like rather than what she does—she does not like gym, math, rain, cold, or the smell of blood. She communicates little with others, blaming it on her inability to "relate well to people."[2] Her interactions with other humans—whether her parents, teachers, or her new friends—suggest that they might not be worth relating to.

Other characters in the book are equally dull. Her dad, Charlie, is withdrawn and awkward, while her mom, Renee, is flighty and easily distracted. Her teachers are stodgy and uninspired. Additionally, none of Bella's human classmates are interesting. Jessica is an endless gossip, and Angela is shy and silent. Bella's male friends have little personality beyond wanting to date her, and they are each rejected as suitable romantic interests. The humans in the novel are not compelling or interesting, and neither is the human world, especially as it is portrayed by the gray, gloomy, rainy Forks. Movies are boring, music does not seem to exist, and even literature does not seem to offer anything new.

In comparison to the uninteresting humans, the vampires offer interest and excitement. The vampires present a perfection usually only found in fiction or in "a scene from a movie."[3] They are described as "devastatingly, inhumanely beautiful."[4] In addition, the vampires smell good and display inhuman strength and formidable intellect. They are wealthy, though the reader is told that they attempt to blend in. At school, they do wear designer clothes, but they refrain from driving their flashy, expensive sports cars, settling instead on a "shiny Volvo" as the least conspicuous option.[5] Most of them have additional supernatural powers. As their most prominent representative, Edward embodies all of these qualities. He is strong and lethal. He dresses impeccably. He drives fast, but safely. In addition to his beautiful appearance, he is fluent in many languages, well read, and conversant on many subjects. He plays the piano with the skill of a professional and composes his own complex music.

> **Argument Two**
>
> The author offers a second supporting claim: "In comparison to the uninteresting humans, the vampires offer interest and excitement." In drawing a comparison between the way in which humans and vampires are represented in the novel, she underscores the ways in which the vampires are represented as superior in every way.

He has amassed several graduate degrees. As Bella repeatedly gushes, he is good at everything. What is more, everything he does seems effortless, as if he were naturally good at it.

Edward's effortlessness in performing a range of activities evokes *sprezzatura*, the most important quality an aristocratic man should possess. According to Baldassare Castiglione's *The Courtier*, a wildly popular sixteenth-century self-help book for aristocrats read for centuries all over Europe, it was *sprezzatura*—or effortlessness in doing everything—that proved a man's nobility and his superiority to others. This quality provided his justification for ruling over others. To obey their social superiors, common people had to believe that their "betters" were literally better than themselves. Aristocrats had to be better at common tasks—better and more cleanly dressed, healthier, prettier, stronger—and they had to master a range of nonessential tasks for which the hardworking commoners had no time. These included elaborate courtly dancing, horse riding, reading and writing literature, playing music, or engaging in witty philosophical conversation. Most important, Castiglione argued, they had to disguise the hard work that inevitably went into practicing this perfection so that it would *seem* effortless. This made the aristocrats appear innately talented and accomplished and of different stock if not a different species than the common folk.

Bella admits that Edward's abilities make her feel "extremely insignificant."[6] Edward does not repudiate this or reveal the amount of work that his "perfection" must have taken; doing so would make him seem human, regular, and weak. <u>On the contrary, Edward uses his *sprezzatura* to manipulate and control others for his benefit.</u> While he and the other Cullens do not kill humans, he does not shy away from exploiting them in every other way when he finds it convenient. Edward listens in on people's conversations when it furthers his personal interests. He sneaks into Bella's bedroom while she is sleeping to snoop around. He uses his allure to muddle her mind and the minds of adults whom he wishes to control.

> **Argument Three**
> Once the contrast has been established, the author has drawn on another structure of understanding, that of the traditional characteristics of the aristocratic character, to suggest that the Cullens are represented as the novel's aristocracy. The third argument states: "On the contrary, Edward uses his *sprezzatura* to manipulate and control others for his benefit." This illustrates how Edward's aristocratic characteristics enable him to control humans.

When Bella seems determined to do something with which he does not agree, he physically restrains her and makes her do his will. He uses his superior abilities to benefit himself and, occasionally, his family. Had any person other than Bella been threatened by a skidding van, for instance, he would have let him or her die without a flinch.

More broadly, the Cullens take advantage of their superior position in human society, giving little in return. With the exception of Carlisle, who works as a doctor at the local hospital, the vampires do not contribute to their community. Though they have already graduated from high school and from college, they choose that route again, instead of finding jobs that use their talents. Repeating school allows these adults to avoid paying taxes on the fairy-tale fortune they have amassed by cheating on the stock market using Alice's visions of the future. This fortune provides them with an enormous economic advantage over everyone else. In their free time, they litter the woods with carcasses of the large animals they

Argument Four

The fourth argument states: "More broadly, the Cullens take advantage of their superior position in human society, giving little in return." The rest of the paragraph gives examples to support this argument.

drain of blood. They put humans in danger by their mere presence. And yet, the reader not only forgives them, the reader admires them.

The Cullens' benevolence in not using their biggest threat—killing humans—masks the many

At their high school, vampires Jasper, Alice, Emmett, Rosalie, and Edward keep to themselves.

Conclusion

This final paragraph is the conclusion of the critique. The author sums up her argument and offers additional implications. By contrasting traditional aristocracy—whose superiority was justified by their responsibility to take care of their subjects—with the Cullens—whose superiority serves only themselves—she further reinforces the thesis.

ways in which they do exploit humanity for their own benefit. When Castiglione wrote about aristocratic perfection, he referred to the responsibility to the ruled subjects, where the right to control also carried an obligation to serve. In telling contrast, the Cullens' pursuit of *sprezzatura* does not lead to responsible leadership but merely to greater control of those around them. The behavior of humans in the novel suggests that they have acclimated, perhaps not consciously, to the underlying social and economic structures that place the Cullens higher than themselves. In the universe of *Twilight*, those with the resources to appear perfect have an uncontested ability to rule those who lack them.

Thinking Critically about *Twilight*

Now it is your turn to assess the critique. Consider these questions:

1. The thesis statement offers an answer to the question of the representation of the vampire's superiority in *Twilight*. What are some other ways to answer this question? Are there other questions you could address using structuralism? How would you answer them?

2. Do you agree with the arguments used to support the thesis statement? Would you use any other elements from the novel to support the thesis? What was the most interesting claim made?

3. The arguments draw on historical materials that have traditionally defined the behavior of aristocracy. Does this information change the way you think about the novel?

Other Approaches

This chapter is one way in which structuralism could approach *Twilight*. Structuralism could equally compare the structure of the human world in the novel and contemporary US society, or contextualize the vampires' behavior within the structures of US law.

Structures of Whiteness

The vampires, who are represented as the most interesting characters, also possess the whitest skin. Bella, as the most compelling human in the novel, also happens to be the palest.

A thesis statement for an essay that discusses the representations of skin color in *Twilight* might be: Through this strategic use of color, *Twilight* affirms larger discriminatory cultural structures, where whiteness is equated with goodness and darkness with evil.

Structuralism, *Twilight*, and Marxism

Structuralists are interested in studying underlying frameworks that drive human experience, including economic and social structures. In this way, structuralism overlaps with Marxist criticism, which deals with similar social and economic concepts. Marxist criticism suggests that obtaining economic power drives human action. As a result, humans are splintered into distinct social classes: the ruling bourgeoisie and the working proletariat. In approaching literature, structuralists and Marxist critics are interested in discerning underlying social rules that govern plotlines.

A thesis statement for an essay exploring these concepts might be: The Cullens' behavior toward humans supports a Marxist concept of social structures, where the Cullens represent the exploitative bourgeoisie and where humans stand as the proletariat.

Meyer, *third from left*, attended a pop arts convention called Comic-Con in 2008 with Twilight Saga actors and the director of *Twilight*.

Chapter 5

An Overview of *New Moon*

After a wonderful summer with Edward, Bella begins to dread her upcoming eighteenth birthday, which will make her older than Edward was when he died and became a vampire. Her unhappiness worsens after a surprise party at the Cullens' home. While opening a stack of presents, Bella cuts herself and Jasper's determination to stop feeding from humans is broken. While Edward, Emmett, and Carlisle stop Jasper's attack, Bella suffers further serious cuts in the shuffle. Bella worries about Edward's rapid change in mood. His former exuberance turns into cold distance.

A few days after the party, Edward reveals that it is time for his family and him to move and that he does not wish for Bella to accompany them. Bella protests and declares, "You can have my soul.

I don't want it without you—it's yours already!"[1] However, Edward negates her offer and informs her that he is tired of pretending to be human. He says, "You're not good for me, Bella."[2] After extracting from her a promise to not "do anything reckless or stupid," he disappears from her life and pledges never to return so that her life could continue as if he "never existed."[3]

Life without Edward

After Edward's departure, Bella lapses into a nearly catatonic state. At night, she suffers from recurring nightmares. During the day, she performs her basic duties at school, work, and home without fully participating in them or communicating with anyone around her, including the reader; the months of October, November, December, and January are merely noted on blank pages in the novel.

In January, Charlie challenges Bella on her inability to deal with her despair. To appease him, Bella invites her friend Jessica to an outing in Port Angeles, where they encounter a foursome of seedy men. Irresistibly drawn to what she recognizes as clear danger, Bella makes two unexpected connections. First, she realizes that she has no desire to keep her promise not to act recklessly. Second, the moment she steps toward the men, she suddenly hears Edward's voice exhorting her to return to safety. Bella is elated and begins plotting dangerous activities that will bring more hallucinations of Edward's voice.

Despite her continued despair, Bella slowly begins recovering. Her pursuit for reckless activities leads her to acquire two motorcycles, which she takes for necessary repair to her mechanically skilled and increasingly attractive friend Jacob Black. She is surprised to find herself laughing in his relaxing company, which provides her with new direction in life and a respite from her nightmares. She is further gratified by the reliable appearance of Edward's voice exhorting her to be safe whenever she rides her motorcycle.

The Werewolf Pack

Bella's recovery is disrupted by the sudden disappearance of Jacob from her life as he suddenly falls ill and then refuses to communicate with her when confronted. Devastated by Jacob's absence and plagued by her persistent despair over Edward, Bella sets out on a hike to find the forest meadow

In the meadow she visited with Edward, Bella encounters vampire Laurent.

she had visited with Edward. There, despite following the cautionary advice provided by Edward's voice, she is attacked by vampire Laurent. He reveals that vampire Victoria is plotting Bella's death as revenge for the death of her mate, James. At the last moment, Bella is saved by five horse-sized wolves that appear and run Laurent off.

Bella suddenly makes connections between her knowledge of Native American legends, her dreams, and hints Jacob has provided. She deduces that Jacob had become the fifth young man in the Quileute tribe to tap into his genetic ability to turn into a werewolf to protect humans from vampire attacks. This werewolf pack not only killed Laurent, but is also pursuing Victoria, who has been trying to approach Forks to kill Bella.

Frequently left alone as Jacob participates in the ongoing hunt for Victoria, Bella eventually decides to refresh her experience of Edward's voice by pursuing the most reckless activity she can devise, and she sets out in a storm to cliff dive. As she expects, Edward's voice is violently opposed to her decision and keeps exhorting her through her subsequent near-drowning experience, from which Jacob saves her at the last minute.

To Italy

Through her second sight, Alice sees Bella's plunge and hastens to Forks to investigate its outcome. Events turn dire when it becomes clear that Edward has found out about Bella's dive. Persuaded that she had committed suicide, Edward sets off for Italy to ask the Volturi, the vampire law enforcers, for death. Bella and Alice travel to Volterra, Italy, where Bella succeeds in intercepting Edward's suicide attempt.

The danger is far from past, however, as the three are captured by the Volturi's guards: Jane, Demetri, and Felix. Aro, Marcus, and Caius, the three Volturi ancients, are convinced that Bella's knowledge of the vampire world is a breach of their rules. They threaten to kill her unless Edward proves clear intent to turn Bella into a vampire. Despite the immediate threat, Edward refuses, but Bella is saved by Alice, who shares with Aro her vision of Bella's future as a vampire.

A New Dilemma

Bella and Edward resume their relationship, despite protests from Charlie and Jacob. Edward explains that his abrupt departure was motivated by his desire to protect Bella from the vampire world and that his declared lack of interest had been a pretense. Bella forgives him, and he pledges never to be parted from her again and to commit suicide shortly after her natural death.

Bella continues to ask for transformation into a vampire, which Edward refuses. Putting the matter to a vote with the Cullens, only Edward and Rosalie vote against her transformation, and Carlisle promises to transform her.

The novel ends with two dilemmas. First,
Edward offers to turn Bella into a vampire himself
if she consents to marry him, a condition that Bella
finds insufferable. Second, Jacob complicates
matters further. He delivers a message from the
werewolves, who have a standing peace treaty with
the Cullens based on the Cullens' vegetarian habits.
The werewolves threaten violent conflict should
the Cullens breach the treaty in biting a human. The
issue of Bella's transformation turns into a question
of war and peace.

The Volturi
ancients

A study of Bella's unconscious in *New Moon* reveals hidden motives for wanting to become a vampire.

6

How to Apply Psychoanalytic Criticism to *New Moon*

No. 2

What Is Psychoanalytic Criticism?

Psychoanalysis, often credited to the Austrian psychologist Sigmund Freud, proposes that humans lack full access to their thoughts. Instead, the conscious mind (the ego) is frequently at odds with the unconscious (the id), which holds each person's instincts, true desires, and impulses. Because many impulsive feelings cannot be expressed in civilized society, the brain uses the conscience (the superego) to mediate between the id and the ego. The superego allows some desires through, while repressing, projecting, or distorting others. Most psychological disorders, Freud theorized, result from the repression of powerful feelings that nevertheless filter into consciousness in unexpected ways.

To access his patients' elusive unconscious, Freud devised psychoanalysis and dreamwork. Psychoanalysis seeks to interpret images, slips of the tongue (sometimes called Freudian slips), and other expressions recurring throughout a patient's talk. Dreamwork, based on the assumption that humans are least influenced by the superego while sleeping, attempts to isolate pervasive images, narratives, and psychological processes in a patient's dreams. While Freud's specific theories were largely discredited, the suggestion that there might be more to thoughts than the conscious mind communicates sparked much research in Western society.

Applying Psychoanalytic Criticism to *New Moon*

For much of *New Moon*, Bella is psychologically unwell and aware of the jarring disjoint between her awareness and her unconscious. As if the readers were the "shrink" she refuses to see, she discusses her feelings, her dreams, and offers tentative interpretations of her condition.[1] She experiences strange hallucinations, wherein her conscience uses Edward's voice to communicate between her conscious mind and unconscious mind in dangerous situations.

The novel provides an extraordinary invitation to engage in thorough psychoanalysis of its primary character. What does Bella really want? An analysis of Bella's dreams, her unconscious slips of the tongue, and her palpable distaste for human life suggests that, despite what she tells the reader about her devastating love for Edward, she wants vampiric strength and immortality above all else.

New Moon begins with a dream that provides immediate access to Bella's conflicted unconscious mind. Careful interpretation of the dream reveals that Bella is uncomfortable with her humanity in general. In this dream, Bella thinks that she sees her grandmother meeting Edward, only to realize that she is seeing her aged self in a mirror. She is

Thesis Statement
The thesis statement in this critique is: "An analysis of Bella's dreams, her unconscious slips of the tongue, and her palpable distaste for human life suggests that, despite what she tells the reader about her devastating love for Edward, she wants vampiric strength and immortality above all else." The thesis suggests that Bella is not fully aware of her unconscious desires.

Argument One
The author has begun supporting the first part of the thesis, which has to do with Bella's unconscious and her discomfort with humanity: "Careful interpretation of the dream reveals that Bella is uncomfortable with her humanity in general." The following text analyzes her dream to point out evidence that illustrates this claim.

mortified. Bella readily admits that this dream is a rebellion of her unconscious against her impending eighteenth birthday. Instead of processing the passing of a year, Bella's unconscious is processing the implications of aging, while immortality, in the guise of Edward, is within arm's reach.

Bella is not worried that she will die but that she will look old—a thought that positively disgusts her. She describes her dream self as "ancient, creased, and withered" and "wasted."[2] Bella's justification of her worry is that she is becoming older than Edward. However, this is not supported by facts. In terms of his true age, Edward is approximately 110 years old. The age Edward pretends to be in human society generally fluctuates between 15 and 30. In the book, he is supposedly 17—an artificially assigned number that does not correspond to any meaningful reality. However, 17 is the age Bella focuses on. Bella's argument of becoming older than Edward seems like a convenient conscious excuse for her general distaste with what it means to be human and gain the negative, but inevitable, appearance of age.

Most of *New Moon* consists of Bella's talk about her debilitating grief over Edward's absence.

<u>Yet, in unfamiliar situations, her</u>
<u>spontaneous remarks—Freudian</u>
<u>slips—suggest that she might</u>
<u>be more devastated by her</u>
<u>ruined chance at vampirism.</u>
On the flight to Volterra, for
instance, Alice reveals that she
has been "debating whether
to just change" Bella into a
vampire herself.[3] At this point
in the narrative, it is unclear
whether Alice and Bella will
reach Edward before he is killed. Additionally,
Bella believes that Edward does not love her; even
if she saves him, she thinks they will not resume
their relationship. Nevertheless, Bella begs Alice
to "do it now! . . . Bite me!"[4] Alice offers a severe
warning by saying, "I'll probably just end up killing
you," but this does not register either, because
Bella would rather die than miss this opportunity
to become a vampire.[5] Here, Bella's desire for
immortality has little to do with Edward, who might
be lost before the airplane lands. In comparison
with her yearning for vampirism, Edward comes in
second.

> **Argument Two**
> The second argument states:
> "Yet, in unfamiliar situations,
> her spontaneous remarks—
> Freudian slips—suggest that
> she might be more devastated
> by her ruined chance at
> vampirism." This argument sets
> up contrast between what the
> main character says she wants
> and what her unconscious
> mind suggests she really
> wants.

Argument Three

The third argument states: "Inasmuch as Bella inadvertently reveals the depth of her desire for immortality, she also periodically—and unexpectedly—identifies the reasons for wishing to be more than the kind of human she is." After arguing that Bella wants to be a vampire above all other things, this argument points out that the text reveals reasons why. The rest of this paragraph and the next provide examples that illustrate Bella's reasons.

Inasmuch as Bella inadvertently reveals the depth of her desire for immortality, she also periodically—and unexpectedly—identifies the reasons for wishing to be more than the kind of human she is. One of these moments surfaces during her confrontation with the intimidating Sam Uley, whom she suspects of bullying Jacob into joining a gang. The violent desire "to be a vampire," she reports, "caught me off guard and knocked the wind out of me. It was the most forbidden of all wishes. . . . That future was lost to me forever, had never really been within my grasp."[6] Here, she not only realizes that she wants to *be* a vampire, but also *why*: she wanted to "gain an advantage over an enemy" and to become "someone who would scare Sam Uley silly."[7] Bella becomes painfully aware of the way in which her small, slender, female body will not register with someone as powerful as Sam. A vampire, by comparison, would be a force to be

reckoned with. These examples give the reader a brief insight into Bella's unconscious motives.

Bella's uncomfortable humanity seems to be the primary fuel for her unconscious desire to become a vampire. Bella's body determines how she functions in society. Several of her suitors, including Edward, take her no to mean yes. Edward treats her like a child, gives her piggyback rides, holds her on his lap, and strokes her hair. She frequently needs to be rescued from harm. And yet, she does not fail to notice the different ways in which diminutive vampire women are treated. She pays close attention, for instance, to the vampire fighters Demetri and Felix's apparent fear of the

Bella is intimidated by Sam Uley and the other werewolves.

"tiny," "fragile" Alice, whose "little arms swung like a child's."[8] Despite Alice's small stature, as a vampire, she is powerful. It is equally not lost on Bella that Jane, another vampire whose "size is . . . insignificant," commands formidable respect. In Jane's presence, "Felix and Demetri relaxed immediately, stepping back from their offensive positions," and "Edward . . . relaxed his position as well . . . in defeat."[9]

> **Conclusion**
> This final paragraph concludes the critique. The author sums up her main arguments and provides additional information about its implications. In stating why Bella is unaware of her own desires, the author underscores the ways in which society can influence an individual consciousness.

As a human, Bella feels nearly powerless. In stark contrast, the vampire world promises unimaginable freedom. Bella longs to become a vampire, whose individual agency is determined by the powers of the mind, not by physical size or gender. Yet, because of the constraints society places on her, she cannot even consciously admit to herself what she wants and why. Instead, these forbidden wishes surface only as solutions to the problem of reconciling her relationship with her supposed true love, Edward.

Thinking Critically about *New Moon*

Now it is your turn to assess the critique. Consider these questions:

1. The thesis statement offers an answer to the question of Bella's true desires. What might be some other ways in which this question could be answered? Are there other questions that could be answered by using psychoanalysis? How would you answer them?

2. Do you agree with the arguments used to support the thesis statement? Would you choose any other examples from the text to support the thesis? To argue against it? What is the most interesting claim the author made?

3. The conclusion briefly reflects on the ways in which society can act as a collective conscience by not allowing individuals to become fully aware of what they truly feel, want, or fear. How does this line of thinking influence your views about the novel?

Other Approaches

Investigating Bella's unconscious is one of many interpretations that psychoanalysis of *New Moon* can produce. Other approaches can focus on the unconscious of other characters, hypothesize about the unconscious dimensions of the author, or psychoanalyze an entire text. As further examples, it can be proposed that, first, Edward functions as Bella's father and, second, that Bella's death instinct causes her to create a fantasy world in which she hears Edward's voice.

Edward as a Father

Bella's childhood was overshadowed by her parents' early divorce and her father's absence. In many ways, Edward fills a father role in Bella's life. He is older, protective, and paternalistic. Edward makes sure Bella takes care of herself, frequently makes decisions for her, takes care of her injuries, teaches her about a world she does not know, and offers to spoil her with material goods.

A thesis for an essay exploring this topic might be: In *New Moon*, rather than the loss of a lover, Bella is debilitated by a second loss of a father.

Freud's Death Instinct

Freud put forth the idea of the human death instinct: that humans are drawn toward self-destructive experiences because they wish to return to the state of nonexistence experienced before birth. His other theories proposed that humans also have a competing drive toward pleasure. These drives create a tension between a desire to live and a desire to die that is displayed in the character of Bella.

A thesis statement for an essay investigating Bella's death instinct might be: Bella desperately wants to live with Edward and wishes to die if she cannot have him. This tension between life and death manifests into hallucinations of Edward's voice and creates a fantasy world in which Edward does desire her.

Rosalie did not want to be transformed into a vampire. She urges Bella to remain human.

7

An Overview of *Eclipse*

New Moon ends with Edward's proposal of
marriage in exchange for Bella's immortality, and
most of *Eclipse* consists of negotiations of the
precise terms. Rosalie and Jasper tell cautionary
tales about their own experiences as humans
transformed into newborn vampires. Rosalie
recounts her own involuntary transformation that
occurred when Carlisle found her dying in the
street after a gang rape brought about by her own
fiancé. Rosalie hopes to persuade Bella not to give
away her humanity. Jasper retells his violent past
as a young vampire used by his creator, Maria, to
lead covens of gullible but powerfully bloodthirsty
newborns into battles in vampire wars. His story
serves as an example of the uneasy existence of a
vampire after transformation.

Taking Rosalie and Jasper's information into account, Bella realizes that there are human experiences—most notably, sex—that she would like to experience before she herself becomes an uncontrollable, bloodthirsty newborn. She brings this request to her negotiations with Edward, only to find him unwilling either to endanger her life by giving full reign to his passion or to have sex before marriage. Eventually, Bella agrees to the marriage in exchange for Edward's promise to try marital sex before her transformation. By the close of the novel, the wedding date is set for August 13, and Alice is put in charge of the preparations.

Love Triangle

Meanwhile, Jacob persists in his attempts to help Bella realize the depth of her feelings for him. Initially, Edward objects to Bella's attempts at friendship with Jacob and actively prevents her from seeing him. Once he realizes Bella's determination to see her friend, Edward relents and vows to "be more reasonable and trust [Bella's] judgment."[1] For his part, Jacob declares his love and his intent to keep "fighting" for Bella "until [her] heart stops beating."[2] Edward accepts the challenge and promises to fight "twice as hard as" Jacob.[3]

For most of the novel, Bella dangles between her two suitors, sometimes literally shuttled between them "like a child being exchanged by custodial guardians."[4] Though she continually notes her need for both Jacob and Edward, Bella consistently asserts her singular preference for Edward. She repeatedly rebuffs Jacob's attempts at intimacy, memorably punching his face and breaking her hand after he kisses her against her will. Eventually, however, Jacob threatens to sacrifice his life to take himself "out of the picture" and tricks Bella into a passionate kiss.[5] Bella recognizes that she loves Jacob deeply, albeit less than she loves Edward, and makes clear her intentions to marry Edward.

Jacob's desperate position is complicated by the fact that, one by one, his fellow werewolves begin imprinting. As Jacob explains to Bella, imprinting is an unconscious biological process wherein a werewolf instinctively focuses all of his attention and affection on a female most likely to carry on the werewolf gene. Akin to—but more powerful than—falling in love, imprinting brings together people who are said to be a "perfect match" for each other.[6] At the outset of *Eclipse*, only the werewolf pack leader Sam had imprinted; he instinctively connected with Emily, the cousin of his former girlfriend, Leah. Leah later joins the pack as the only female werewolf in the tribe's memory. As *Eclipse* unfolds, more of the werewolves imprint, driving Jacob to worry about his own agency in determining his future. His desperate pursuit of Bella is as much an assertion of his independence from the biological imperative as an expression of actual desire.

Vampire Battle

Meanwhile, Victoria provides an ever-present danger to the helpless human Bella. Resolved on revenging her mate's death, Victoria sets an elaborate plan to attack the Cullens and kill Bella. She makes several forays into Forks to test the Cullens' preparedness, the werewolves' capabilities, and the loopholes in Alice's supernatural foresight. Together with a new companion, Riley, she creates an army of newborns in Seattle, where they wreak havoc. The threat, slowly pieced together by the protagonists, unifies the Cullens and the werewolves.

This new alliance is effective in destroying the newborns in the battle that unfolds at the conclusion of the novel. Separated from the rest, Edward, werewolf Seth, and Bella encounter and destroy Victoria and Riley. The victory over Victoria's army is accentuated by the unexpected visit of the Volturi guard, a select group of vampire fighters led by Jane. They are evidently disappointed that the Cullens were unharmed in the attack, but they are reassured that Bella will be transformed. They depart after destroying Bree, who had surrendered to the Cullens and was the lone newborn survivor of the attack.

A fan reads *Eclipse* before a midnight viewing of the movie in 2010.

Much of the plot of *Eclipse* centers on a love triangle between Edward, Bella, and Jacob.

8

How to Apply Queer Theory to *Eclipse*

No.2

What Is Queer Theory?

Queer theory is sometimes referred to as sexuality studies, gay studies, or gay/lesbian/bisexual/transgender (GLBT) studies. Queer theory questions heteronormativity, or the pressure that society places on people to engage in and identify through intimate relationships with people of the opposite sex. As a critical approach, queer theory is attuned to textual representations of relationships that are between persons of the same sex.

Queer critics are equally interested in how sexuality is understood, categorized, institutionalized, and enforced in a society. Far from objecting to heterosexuality, queer theory focuses on the use of heterosexuality as a way to influence and direct individual life choices and self-identification. Because there is not a single same-sex relationship represented in *Eclipse*, one might think that there is nothing to interpret through queer theory. It is important to consider, however, that even an absence means something. If fiction generally represents the world, then a partial representation that denies the existence of a sizeable proportion of the population is worth noting.

As far as *Eclipse* is concerned, then, the only relationships worth considering are heterosexual. Queer theory would survey all the heterosexual relationships—whether intimate, sexual, or close friendships—that *Eclipse* does portray. How are they represented? Is the reader to accept some of them as more important than others? How is this importance determined? Which relationships are defined as different from the norm? What does the novel suggest that the reader learn from these nonnormative examples? Finally, queer theory would ask, how do all of these models fit with the accepted normative boundaries of today's society? Does the novel provoke the reader to think critically, or does it merely reinforce well-accepted boundaries of normativity?

Applying Queer Theory to *Eclipse*

Pursuing questions of relationships within the world of *Eclipse* leads to the conclusion that, despite an emphasis on freedom of choice, the protagonists have no choice when it comes to determining their own life paths. Instead, Meyer demonstrates that there is only one predetermined *right* course of action for Bella and any person faced with the prospect of determining the worth of various relationships. This choice is to follow the rules and value traditional marriage rooted in irresistible, biologically determined heterosexual desire.

The werewolves' communal relationship is intensely intimate. They rely on each other implicitly, thereby creating a community where individual members cooperate with, support, and defend each other to the point of bodily harm. They have virtually no secrets from each other. Nevertheless, these significant relationships (and all

---

Thesis Statement

The thesis statement in this critique is: "Instead, Meyer demonstrates that there is only one predetermined *right* course of action for Bella and any person faced with the prospect of determining the worth of various relationships. This choice is to follow the rules and value traditional marriage rooted in irresistible, biologically determined heterosexual desire." This thesis offers an answer to the questions: Do *Eclipse*'s positively portrayed characters have a free choice when it comes to picking a romantic partner? Is free choice a good thing?

other ties the werewolves have to their families, friends, or communities) are decidedly secondary to imprinting, wherein a werewolf finds the "right" heterosexual mate. As Jacob explains, "it's . . . like gravity moves. When you see *her*, suddenly it's not the earth holding you here any more. She does."[1] This imperative imprinting impulse is determined, the characters report, by the biological suitability of the prospective partner to carry on the werewolf gene to the next generation. In this regard, the werewolves are helpless victims of biology, which supplies appropriate desire when a proper biological target is found.

This lack of choice raises a host of potential additional problems that the novel ignores. Does biological suitability equal a compatibility of personalities? Of cultural values? Is intense sexual desire enough to ensure successful long-term partnership? Beyond the inability of the werewolves to choose on whom they will imprint, imprinting raises significant questions about the agency of each imprinting target. Is it inevitable that the chosen woman will return the offered affection? The novel shuts down speculation on the subject by equating free choice with heteronormativity. After all, when discussing a woman's choice in imprinting, Meyer challenges, "Why wouldn't she choose him, in the end? He'll be her perfect match. Like he was designed for her alone."[2] The inevitable right choice, here, is paradoxically no choice at all: a sufficiently loved person will, *of course*, return the affection; there are no other options.

The central love triangle similarly suggests that choosing a partner is more harmful than falling helplessly into heterosexual love. It is clear that Bella's decision between Edward and Jacob has little to do with her choice: as she comes to understand, her connection to Edward is addictive "like a drug" and very much like the werewolves' imprinting.[3] As she tells Jacob, "It's like Sam and Emily, Jake—I never

Argument One

Having investigated the werewolves' imprinting as an example of biologically determined heterosexual desire that supports the thesis, the author articulates the first argument: "The inevitable right choice, here, is paradoxically no choice at all: a sufficiently loved person will, of *course*, return the affection; there are no other options." The author placed her argument after her examples so that the logic of the argument would be clear.

Argument Two

Looking closely at the central love relationships in the novel, the author illustrates that they are as devoid of actual choice as the werewolves' imprinting. She articulates this point in the second supporting argument: "The central love triangle similarly suggests that choosing a partner is more harmful than falling helplessly into heterosexual love."

had a choice."[4] Bella's love for Jacob is similarly marked by helplessness and lack of choice. To realize that Jacob is her "soul mate," Bella has to be manipulated into kissing him.[5] It is Jacob's passionate anger that makes her recognize that she loves him and that—as she sees in a momentary vision—their relationship would result in the birth of "two small, black-haired children."[6] Bella's subsequent marriage to Edward is not a choice, but it is merely obedience to the desire that makes her helpless.

<table>
<tr><td>

Argument Three

The author's third argument is: "In *Eclipse*, actual free choice emerges as a considerable threat to the peaceful fabric of society." The author supports this argument with examples from the novel that illustrate the perils of free choice in relationships.

</td></tr>
</table>

In *Eclipse*, actual free choice emerges as a considerable threat to the peaceful fabric of society. In contrast to this successful heteronormativity, which requires inevitability and lack of choice, the novel provides examples of relationships that are heterosexual but perilously founded on personal choice. The novel dooms all of these relationships to violent ends, as if to suggest that free choice in the consideration of a potential partner poses a threat to society.

Two relationships are presented to Bella as examples of wrong relationship choices: Rosalie's arranged engagement and Jasper's cooperative arrangement with Maria. The results are rape, war, senseless procreation, and the murder of one's offspring. Because Rosalie chose to marry for status rather than falling in love hopelessly, she dies. Jasper's relationship with Maria, absent the helplessness of procreative force, similarly results in disenchantment, violence, and desertion. Finally, the most prominent choice-based relationship—that of Victoria's family—constitutes the most prominent threat of the entire novel. After the death of James, Victoria's partnership with Riley and the subsequent creation of vampire offspring are matters of choice rather than of a helpless imprinting. As such, the relationship has no chance of surviving, and the novel denies it a possibility of success. From the start, the relationship is depicted as inevitably deceitful, manipulative, vengeful, exploitive, and bent on the general destruction of Bella, those who protect her, and any vampire children who happen to fall in battle.

Eclipse provides only one "right" model of happiness found in one model of a perfect

Conclusion

Here, the author concludes the critique by summarizing her arguments. By pointing out that in the world of *Eclipse* free choice is a farce, the author invites reflection on how free choice functions in today's society.

relationship: a biologically driven heterosexual marriage where neither party has the agency to choose his or her partner. In this context, nothing else seems to matter. The questions of shared values, interpersonal relations, or compatibility promise to be magically resolved. As Bella explains to Edward in *Eclipse*'s conclusion, "I *am* going to do this right . . . I'm following all the rules."[7] *Eclipse* might suggest that free choice is a farce, a rhetoric that is ever present but never borne out by any of the protagonists. On the contrary, authentic free choice seems to pose an ever-present threat.

Thinking Critically about *Eclipse*

Now it is your turn to assess the critique. Consider these questions:

1. The thesis statement answers questions about the free will of characters in the novel. What are some other ways to answer these questions? Are there other questions that could be answered using queer theory? How would you go about articulating and answering them?

2. Do you agree with the arguments used to support the thesis statement? Which one do you find the most interesting? Would you use any other arguments to support this thesis? Are there arguments you could make to argue against the offered thesis?

3. The conclusion broadens the consideration beyond the novel. What do you think is the role of society in determining the scope of romantic choices a person should have?

Other Approaches

There are many ways to interpret *Eclipse* using queer theory. Other interpretations could question the parameters of the relationship between Edward and Jacob or the purposes of vampire heterosexual coupling.

Edward and Jacob

In the 1980s, Eve Kosofsky Sedgwick introduced a concept in her book *Between Men: English Literature and Male Homosocial Desire*. This phrase *male homosocial desire* refers to dominant male bonds and relationships. She claimed that while homosociality is different from homosexuality, the two concepts are on the same continuum. Furthermore, Sedgwick referred to the work of René Girard, who studied the nature of love triangles. With these concepts in mind, *Eclipse* offers an interesting pairing of Edward with Jacob. Throughout the novel, as Edward and Jacob fight for Bella's affection, they come to dominate each other's private thoughts. Edward even states, "If it weren't for the fact that we were natural enemies and that you're also trying to steal away the reason for my existence, I might actually like you."[8]

A thesis statement for this approach might be: The main tension in *Eclipse* is created not by Bella's decision of which man to choose, but by the process of the two men determining the parameters of their relationship to each other.

Vampire Marriage

The novel's general organization of protagonists into heterosexual couples extends to all three represented species. Heteronormativity is explained for humans and werewolves as a procreative necessity that ensures the passing on of all the best genes to the next generation. However, no such requirement exists for the vampires. Nevertheless, most vampires are tidily organized into married, sexually active couples. Queer theory would ask why. Since the vampires are not able to procreate, there is no biological imperative to form long-term heterosexual couples.

A thesis statement for an essay exploring this topic might state: *Eclipse* is unable or unwilling to consider alternatives to heteronormativity that might include imagining spending one's eternity differently, whether it be in friendships, communities, long- or short- term serial monogamies, same-sex relationships, or independently alone.

Breaking Dawn, the fourth book in The Twilight Saga, was released at midnight on August 2, 2008.

An Overview of
Breaking Dawn

Breaking Dawn begins with Bella and Edward's long-anticipated wedding. Though Bella has been resistant to getting married, she realizes on the wedding day that being married is right for her and that her world settles "into its right position."[1] The event is successful, and even Jacob returns from his roaming in werewolf form to congratulate the happy couple. The newlyweds depart for their honeymoon on Isle Esme, an island the Cullens own off the coast of Brazil. There, they consummate their marriage. While the readers do not see the act, they witness Bella waking up bruised head to toe from lovemaking with the statuesque Edward. Edward is contrite and vows never to attempt physical intimacy again until Bella's transformation to vampire. Bella is elated, saying she has "never been better."[2] Bella, nevertheless, persuades Edward to try again, and within days, she finds herself in a mysteriously accelerated pregnancy.

A New Werewolf Clan

At this point, the novel makes an unexpected turn to Jacob's perspective, through whose eyes the reader sees the unfolding events. The leader of the werewolf pack, Sam, decides that the unknown creature Bella carries within her is a threat to humans and plots to lead his pack to attack the Cullens. Drawing on his genetic predispositions as alpha wolf, Jacob breaks away from his pack to warn and protect the vampires. He is followed by werewolves Seth, who had formed a friendship with Edward in *Eclipse*, and Seth's sister, Leah, who joins Jacob to escape the collective mind-intimacy of a pack led by her ex-boyfriend.

The Vampire Baby

As the pregnancy rapidly progresses, Bella's health deteriorates. It is clear that her life is in danger. Edward, Jacob, and Carlisle repeatedly and emphatically try to persuade her to have an abortion, but Bella (with Rosalie's help) refuses all options in favor of carrying the baby to term. Bella counts on Edward to turn her into a vampire once the child is removed from her womb—something Jacob calls an "emergency vampirization."[3] Unexpectedly, her placenta detaches, and through a grisly and bloody birth, Reneesme (Nessie) is born. Many of Bella's bones are broken in the delivery. Blinded by his grief over Bella's suffering and what he sees as her impending death, Jacob sets off to destroy the creature he holds responsible, the infant Nessie. Instead, he imprints on the infant.

As Bella undergoes the excruciating burning pain of vampirization that eventually stops her heart, the novel returns to her perspective. She awakens to a new world, realizing that she "found her true place" and that she "had been born to be a vampire."[4] She is "indisputably beautiful."[5] Finally, she is graceful, incredibly powerful, intellectually capable, and far more aware of the world than she ever had been as a "half-blind" human.[6] She surprises everyone by her immense self-control, unusual for newborn vampires whose dominant characteristics tend to be violent mood swings and uncontrollable thirst for human blood. She is "euphoric" in her new life as she balances her love for Edward, Nessie, and Jacob.[7] However, Bella worries for her daughter who continues to grow at breakneck speed. Within three months of her birth, Nessie physically resembles "a big one-year-old, or a small two-year-old."[8] Intellectually, she is far more advanced, reading Tennyson to her mother at bedtime.

Alice's Vision

The collective happiness is shattered by Alice's unexpected vision of the Volturi, who have set out to destroy the Cullens under the pretense that Nessie is an illegally created immortal, vampirized child. Alice deals a second blow by her sudden departure with Jasper, leaving the rest to believe that their doom is imminent. Resolved not to give up, the Cullens gather many vampire friends to witness Nessie's interspecies origins and her rapid development. The Cullens hope that their testimony regarding how she grows and how she is capable of abiding by vampire law might stop the Volturi's resolve.

Suspecting that the Volturi will welcome any excuse to obliterate them, however, the Cullens, their friends, and the werewolves prepare for a

fight. As Bella trains with the visiting vampires, she discovers that she has immense shielding powers, allowing her to protect her loved ones from the

Vampire Alice's visions of the future help the Cullen side prepare for the Volturi's arrival.

mind-destroying superpowers of their opponents. In addition to practicing her newfound ability, she makes practical arrangements that would allow Jacob and Nessie to escape the war and, hopefully, be reunited with Alice and Jasper abroad.

A War Avoided

Once the Volturi arrive, it becomes apparent that their goal is to persuade those on the Cullen side with the most precious superpowers to join the Volturi ranks. Once Nessie's interspecies identity becomes clear, they continue to look for potential infringements for which the Cullens could be punished, finally settling on the potential threat of Nessie's uncertain future.

In the ensuing largely verbal altercation, the extent of Bella's shielding power becomes apparent, incapacitating the Volturi's most effective offensive fighters. When the clearly exhibited defensive and destructive potential among the many talented vampires and wolves on the Cullen side make the Volturi pause, they halt completely after the unexpected arrival of Alice. With Alice is Nahuel, an interspecies immortal conceived similarly to Nessie. He recounts his own history and lays to rest any questions about Nessie's future. Thwarted in their purpose and awed by the Cullens' show of power, the Volturi depart without a fight.

The series ends with Bella and Edward settling into domestic life in their fairy-tale, stone-forest cottage.

Bella and Edward's changing relationship highlights issues related to gender criticism.

How to Apply Gender Criticism to *Breaking Dawn*

No.2

What Is Gender Criticism?

Gender criticism includes feminist and masculinity studies. As a critical approach, gender criticism investigates the ways in which texts represent anything that has to do with gender. This approach looks at the way in which texts link particular biological bodies (sex) with a set of presumably appropriate behaviors (gender roles) and how these gender roles determine what characters can and cannot do in their societies. Gender critics seek to understand how specific gender roles are assigned. Are some behaviors biologically determined? Which behaviors are learned from society? And, if society instills particular gendered preferences, who stands to benefit from them? Who is limited by them?

In general, those who employ gender studies have emphatically argued for the necessity of equal agency of all people regardless of their gender. As such, gender critics probe into structures where gender roles inhibit an individual's agency to develop all his or her abilities and become a productive member of society.

Applying Gender Criticism to *Breaking Dawn*

Most of the criticism of The Twilight Saga has come from scholars of gender, who have protested the inherent inequality between Bella and Edward. In the first three novels, Edward has most of the agency in their relationship. He always knows what Bella should do and manipulates her accordingly. In comparison, Bella obediently follows traditional feminine roles. She cooks and cleans for her father, despises math, and avoids sports. In this aspect, *Breaking Dawn* offers a new universe. As a vampire, Bella becomes Edward's equal in every way. Once they are of the same species, each contributes according to his or her specific gifts and abilities, but their contributions are not stereotypically masculine for Edward or feminine for Bella. Additionally, the novel does not do this only with Bella and Edward. In the supernatural world of the Cullens, good vampires exhibit unwavering respect for every member of their extended international community, trusting their respective individual abilities regardless of their correlation to traditional gender roles. The novel illustrates that gender equality is essential for the survival of a free, democratic society.

The novel disrupts traditional gender roles before Bella's vampirization to underscore the importance of responsible self-determination over limiting social norms. Though Bella meticulously performed expected gender roles while living with her father, once she is married, she and Edward determine their roles organically, with a view to each other's interests and needs. Edward does most of the cooking, although he does not eat human food

Thesis Statement

The thesis statement in this critique is: "The novel illustrates that gender equality is essential for the survival of a free, democratic society." The thesis offers an answer to the question: How is gender represented in *Breaking Dawn*?

Argument One

The author immediately begins supporting the thesis. The first supporting argument states: "The novel disrupts traditional gender roles before Bella's vampirization to underscore the importance of responsible self-determination over limiting social norms." The rest of the paragraph gathers evidence from the novel that supports this argument.

himself. Throughout the novel, Edward regularly provides for the nutritional needs of nonhumans at the Cullens' house, including the allied werewolves, suggesting that men are not only as capable as women in the kitchen, but that they may derive enjoyment from cooking. Despite traditional social norms that suggest it is inappropriate for women to openly express sexual desire, in their marriage, both Bella and Edward communicate their need for sexual union as something that is natural for both partners. It is generally Bella who argues for more frequent consummation of their desire for each other. Most important, the novel emphasizes Bella's choice when it comes to her pregnancy. Though many of the characters do not agree with her choice, they do not assume control of her body to force her into an option with which she does not agree.

Once Nessie is born and Bella is vampirized, the inherent need for equality between partners becomes even more explicitly articulated. Both Bella and Edward function

---

Argument Two

The author continues building the overarching argument by presenting the second supporting claim: "Once Nessie is born and Bella is vampirized, the inherent need for equality between partners becomes even more explicitly articulated." Here, the author points out that gender is not the main factor for determining a character's behaviors or actions.

as stay-at-home parents who take care of their daughter equally. The doubt that Edward frequently expressed about Bella's decisions prior to her vampirization evaporates. In *Breaking Dawn*, he consistently respects her choices, even when it "goes against the grain" of his gendered upbringing.[1] As difficult as it is for him to watch his wife hunt a mountain lion, he does not interfere, allowing her to learn the full extent of her powers. He does not question or inquire into her independent preparations for the confrontation with the Volturi, implicitly trusting her judgment. When she argues for the need to "learn to fight," Edward agrees to her decision to train in vampire combat.[2]

As a vampire, Bella is no longer represented as explicitly gendered. While she is described as "indisputably beautiful," so are the rest of the Cullens, including the men.[3] She is as smart, graceful, and perceptive. As a newborn, she is more physically strong than the most masculine of the Cullens' fighters, Emmett, and she effortlessly beats him in an arm-wrestling match. Most important, she finds and improves her own unique individual talents that eventually contribute to the preservation of her society. Once she is on equal species footing

> **Argument Three**
>
> The next supporting claim turns to looking at the way that gender equality is an essential trait of the community on the novel's "good" side: "The novel represents this equality as absolutely essential to the Cullen side's eventual victory over the Volturi." Here, the author points out that equality is portrayed as the necessary building block of a successful society.

with the Cullens, she becomes their undisputed equal in abilities and accomplishments. Her sense of "rightness" at being a vampire comes explicitly from the fact that she fits in as an equal.[4]

The novel represents this equality as absolutely essential to the Cullen side's eventual victory over the Volturi. The ability and willingness to fight is split evenly between male and female vampires. At the forefront of the eagerness to fight is Emmett, whose masculine traits tend toward the confrontational throughout the novels. This eagerness is also shown in Tanya, the Alaskan relative who seems eager to join the "suicide mission."[5] A similar gender balance is exhibited on the other end of the spectrum, where both men (Carlisle, most prominently) and women (Siobhan, a friend from Ireland) use their powers to contribute to a peaceful outcome. Along with many others, Bella is ambivalent, wavering between fear and powerful "bloodlust" which causes her to want to fight.[6] Despite this bloodlust, Bella is one of

The vampires' abilities are displayed in the confrontation at the end of the novel. Aro, one of the Volturi ancients, can read minds through touch.

the primary agents who contribute to the peaceful resolution of the conflict.

While the eventual retreat of the Volturi is represented as the result of egalitarian collective action on the Cullen side, it specifically underscores the contributions of female vampires as if to remind the reader that women's contributions are no less important to society than men's. The men certainly do their share. Carlisle does the bulk of public speaking, Edward works overtime in reading the minds of the key Volturi opponents, and Garret (a visiting nomad) delivers a passionate speech. It is the women's contributions, however, that deliver the decisive blows. In addition to Siobhan's powerful willing of a peaceful outcome, her companion Maggie uses her ability to "hear the truth" to sift through the Volturi's statements.[7] The Amazonian vampire Zafrina stands ready to incapacitate the opponents through her skill of projecting visions, and the Alaskan Kate readies her ability to shock anyone who touches her.

Bella's own ability to shield her entire company from the mind-powers of the Volturi is proclaimed to be the decisive factor in the Volturi's retreat, so much so that the Cullens lay the victory almost solely at Bella's feet. Finally, it is indisputably Alice's strategic use of her visions to determine the route toward victory, and everyone else's unquestioning acceptance of her directions, that make the victory possible.

In *Breaking Dawn*, had the women been limited by traditional gender norms to the domestic space, the Volturi would have decimated the Cullen side. In this aspect, the novel is unequivocal. Everyone is equally responsible for the society they inhabit, contributing to the best of their individual— rather than gendered—abilities.

Conclusion
Here, the author concludes the critique by summarizing her arguments and broadening the view into a consideration of gender as a building block of society.

Thinking Critically about *Breaking Dawn*

Now it is your turn to assess the critique. Consider these questions:

1. The thesis statement answers the question of the importance of gender representation in *Breaking Dawn*. What are some other ways to answer this question? Are there other questions that could be articulated and answered by using gender criticism? How would you ask and answer them?

2. Do you agree with the arguments used to support the thesis? Is there other evidence you think should be considered? Would this evidence strengthen or weaken the thesis? How?

3. The conclusion broadens the critique into a consideration of the role of gender in everyday life. What do you think this role is? What do you think it should be? Why?

Other Approaches

The previous argument is only one possible interpretation a gender studies approach might generate. Other interpretations could, for example, look at the representation of femininity in the werewolf Leah, or investigate the gendered structure of the Volturi society.

Freaky Leah

As the only female werewolf, Leah represents an interesting point of analysis. On the one hand, she is an equal of the werewolves in ability to hunt and protect and superior in speed. On the other hand, she is ostracized by her pack because of her gender, as the male werewolves are unnerved by her "female stuff."[8] Furthermore, she herself is extremely ambivalent about her new role, despairing over the possibility that she is a "genetic dead end" because none of the male werewolves have imprinted on her.[9] She calls herself a "freak — the girlie wolf — good for nothing else."[10]

A thesis statement for an essay analyzing Leah might state: Through the novel's plotline, the reader may conclude that women's primary strength is their ability to reproduce.

Patriarchal Volturi

In comparison to the Cullens' egalitarian society in which everyone voluntarily contributes according to his or her best abilities, the Volturi represent a coercive hierarchical patriarchy. As the oldest males, the three who rule, Aro, Caius, and Marcus, are vampire equivalents of patriarchs. Unlike the women on the Cullen side, the Volturi women, although presumably as old and wise as their husbands, are distinct nonentities. Nameless and faceless, they hunch in protected positions at the end of the Volturi formation. It is also important to note that the Volturi rule through coercion. The obedience of their guard is secured through a magical bond bestowed by one of their number, who can "make someone feel bonded to the Volturi . . . to want to please them" so that the "guard obey their masters . . . with almost lover-like devotion."[11]

A thesis statement for an essay investigating gender roles in the Volturi society might state: In this representation of the Volturi army as a mindless mass manipulated into obedience, the novel suggests that traditional patriarchy is decidedly unnatural.

You Critique It

Now that you have learned about different critical theories and how to apply them to literature, are you ready to perform your own critique? You have read that this type of evaluation can help you look at literature in a new way and make you pay attention to certain issues you may not have otherwise recognized. So, why not use one of the critical theories profiled in this book to consider a fresh take on your favorite book?

First, choose a theory and the book you want to analyze. Remember that the theory is a springboard for asking questions about the work.

Next, write a specific question that relates to the theory you have selected. Then you can form your thesis, which should provide the answer to that question. Your thesis is the most important part of your critique and offers an argument about the work based on the tenets, or beliefs, of the theory you are applying. Recall that the thesis statement typically appears at the very end of the introductory paragraph of your essay. It is usually only one sentence long.

After you have written your thesis, find evidence to back it up. Good places to start are in the work itself or in journals or articles that discuss what other people have said about it. Since you are critiquing a book, you may also want to read about the author's life so you can get a sense of what factors may have affected the creative process. This can be especially useful if working within historical, biographical, or psychological criticism.

Depending on which theory you are applying, you can often find evidence in the book's language, plot, or character development. You should also explore parts of the book that seem to disprove your thesis and create an argument against them. As you do this, you might want to address what other critics have written about the book. Their quotes may help support your claim.

Before you start analyzing a work, think about the different arguments made in this book. Reflect on how evidence supporting the thesis was presented. Did you find that some of the techniques used to back up the arguments were more convincing than others? Try these methods as you prove your thesis in your own critique.

When you are finished writing your critique, read it over carefully. Is your thesis statement understandable? Do the supporting arguments flow logically, with the topic of each paragraph clearly stated? Can you add any information that would present your readers with a stronger argument in favor of your thesis? Were you able to use quotes from the book, as well as from other critics, to enhance your ideas?

Did you see the work in a new light?

Timeline

1973 Stephenie Morgan (later Meyer) is born on December 24 in Hartford, Connecticut.

1978 The Morgan family relocates from Connecticut to Phoenix, Arizona.

2003 Meyer starts writing *Twilight* in June.

2005 *Twilight* is published on October 5. It reaches the *New York Times* best-seller list of children's literature within a month.

2006 *New Moon* is published on August 21 and immediately makes the *New York Times* best-seller list in children's literature.

2007 *Eclipse* is published on August 7 and catapults to numerous best-seller lists.

Meyer's "Hell on Earth," a short story, is published in a teen anthology *Prom Nights from Hell*.

2008 *The Host* is published on May 6 and debuts at number one on the *New York Times* best-seller list.

Breaking Dawn is published on August 2; more than 1.3 million copies sell that day.

The film version of *Twilight* is released on November 21.

Meyer is included in *Time* magazine's list of the 100 most influential people.

Twilight is the best-selling book of the year.

1992

Morgan graduates from high school in Scottsdale, Arizona.

1997

Morgan graduates with an English degree from Brigham Young University.

Morgan marries Christian "Pancho" Meyer and becomes Stephenie Meyer.

2009

The film version of *New Moon* is released on November 20.

Meyer ranks twenty-sixth on the *Forbes* list of the 100 most powerful celebrities.

2010

The Short Second Life of Bree Tanner is published on June 5.

The film version of *Eclipse* is released on June 30.

coven
A group of vampires.

dreamwork
Within psychoanalysis, the interpretation of dreams to determine a person's true feelings, desires, and fears.

ego
The conscious part of the human psyche, wherein a person is aware of the self and his or her identity.

gender
The social character of being male or female.

gender role
A public expression of behaviors ascribed to being male or female.

heteronormativity
A social force that requires that individuals identify primarily through their pairing with a partner of the opposite sex.

heterosexuality
A form of sexuality involving two partners of the opposite sex.

hierarchy
A system of organizing something on a vertical scale or order where some things are defined as better or more valuable than others.

homosexuality
> A form of sexuality involving two partners of the
> same sex.

id
> In psychoanalysis, the unconscious part of the
> human self. According to Freud, this is the part of
> the human psyche that contains a person's instincts,
> true desires, and impulses; this part of the psyche is
> not easily accessible to the conscious mind.

imprinting
> In the *Twilight* novels, an unconscious biological
> process in which a wolf focuses on a female most
> likely to carry on the wolf gene.

patriarchy
> A method of social organization in which males
> primarily have power.

sex
> Categorization of human beings according to
> biology: male or female.

sprezzatura
> A concept put forth by Baldassare Castiglione
> declaring that a noble must appear to be effortlessly
> good at everything he does.

superego
> The part of human psyche that acts as a conscience,
> mediating between the unconscious (the id) and
> consciousness (the ego).

Bibliography of Works and Criticism

Important Works

Twilight, 2005

New Moon, 2006

Eclipse, 2007

"Hell on Earth," a short story included in *Prom Nights
from Hell*, 2007

Breaking Dawn, 2008

The Host, 2008

*The Short Second Life of Bree Tanner: An Eclipse
Novella*, 2010

Critical Discussions

Ayers, David. *Literary Theory: A Reintroduction*.
Oxford: Blackwell, 2008. Print.

Barry, Peter. *Beginning Theory: An Introduction to
Literary and Cultural Theory*. Third ed. Manchester:
Manchester UP, 2009. Print.

Hopkins, Ellen, ed. *A New Dawn: Your Favorite Authors
on Stephenie Meyer's* Twilight *Series*. Dallas, TX:
BenBella, 2008. Print.

Palmer, Donald. *Structuralism and Poststructuralism for
Beginners*. Danbury, CT: For Beginners, 2007. Print.

Parker, Robert Dale. *How to Interpret Literature:
Critical Theory for Literary and Cultural Studies*.
Oxford: Oxford UP, 2008. Print.

Resources

Selected Bibliography

Housel, Rebecca, and J. Jeremy Wisnewski, eds. Twilight *and Philosophy: Vampires, Vegetarians, and the Pursuit of Immortality*. Hoboken, NJ: John Wiley & Sons, 2009. Print.

Meyer, Stephenie. *Breaking Dawn*. New York: Little, 2008. Print.

Meyer, Stephenie. *Eclipse*. New York: Little, 2007. Print.

Meyer, Stephenie. *New Moon*. New York: Little, 2006. Print.

Meyer, Stephenie. *Twilight*. New York: Little, 2005. Print.

Further Readings

Krohn, Katherine. *Stephenie Meyer: Dreaming of Twilight*. Minneapolis, MN: Twenty-First Century Books, 2011. Print.

Shapiro, Marc. *Stephenie Meyer: The Unauthorized Biography of the Creator of the Twilight Saga*. New York: St. Martin's Griffin, 2010. Print.

Ward, Ivan. *Introducing Psychoanalysis*. Toronto: Totem, 2001. Print.

Web Links

To learn more about critiquing the works of Stephenie Meyer, visit ABDO Publishing Company online at **www.abdopublishing.com**. Web sites about the works of Stephenie Meyer are featured on our Book Links page. These links are routinely monitored and updated to provide the most current information available.

For More Information
Science Fiction & Fantasy Writers of America
www.sfwa.org

This organization hosts awards, gives tips on writing and getting published, and offers support for those who write or are interested in science fiction and fantasy writing.

Stephenie Meyer's Official Web Site
www.stepheniemeyer.com

Fans can read a biography of Stephenie Meyer and updates on her upcoming projects. This site also contains a rough draft of *Midnight Sun*, an incomplete draft of the novel *Twilight* from Edward's perspective.

Source Notes

Chapter 1. Introduction to Critiques
None.

Chapter 2. A Closer Look at Stephenie Meyer
1. "Bio." *The Official Website of Stephenie Meyer*. N.p, n.d. 8 Jan. 2010. Web.
2. Lev Grossman. "Stephenie Meyer: A New J.K. Rowling?" *Time*. Time Inc., 24 Apr. 2008. Web. 10 Jan. 2010.

Chapter 3. An Overview of *Twilight*
None.

Chapter 4. How to Apply Structuralism to *Twilight*
1. Lois Tyson. *Critical Theory Today: A User-Friendly Guide*. New York: Garland, 1999. Print. 198.
2. Stephenie Meyer. *Twilight*. New York: Little, 2005. Print. 10.
3. Ibid. 41.
4. Ibid. 19.
5. Ibid. 14.
6. Ibid. 326.

Chapter 5. An Overview *New Moon*

1. Stephenie Meyer. *New Moon*. New York: Little, 2006. Print. 69.

2. Ibid. 70.

3. Ibid. 71.

Chapter 6. How to Apply Psychoanalytic Criticism to *New Moon*

1. Stephenie Meyer. *New Moon*. New York: Little, 2006. Print. 96.

2. Ibid. 6.

3. Ibid. 436.

4. Ibid.

5. Ibid. 437.

6. Ibid. 263.

7. Ibid.

8. Ibid. 455.

9. Ibid. 456.

Chapter 7. An Overview of *Eclipse*

1. Stephenie Meyer. *Eclipse*. New York: Little, 2007. Print. 190.

2. Ibid. 330.

3. Ibid. 341.

4. Ibid. 318.

5. Ibid. 523.

6. Ibid. 176.

Source Notes Continued

Chapter 8. How to Apply Queer Theory to *Eclipse*

1. Stephenie Meyer. *Eclipse*. New York: Little, 2007. Print. 176.

2. Ibid.

3. Ibid. 599.

4. Ibid. 600.

5. Ibid. 599.

6. Ibid. 529.

7. Ibid. 619-620.

8. Ibid. 503.

Chapter 9. An Overview of *Breaking Dawn*

1. Stephenie Meyer. *Breaking Dawn*. New York: Little, 2008. Print. 49.

2. Ibid. 88.

3. Ibid. 191.

4. Ibid. 524.

5. Ibid. 403.

6. Ibid. 391.

7. Ibid. 527.

8. Ibid. 529.

Chapter 10. How to Apply Gender Criticism to
Breaking Dawn

1. Stephenie Meyer. *Breaking Dawn*. New York: Little, 2008. Print. 423.

2. Ibid. 574.

3. Ibid. 403.

4. Ibid. 524.

5. Ibid. 593.

6. Ibid. 729.

7. Ibid. 660.

8. Ibid. 317.

9. Ibid.

10. Ibid. 319.

11. Ibid. 318.

Index

About the Author

Marcela Kostihova is an associate professor of English at Hamline University in St. Paul, Minnesota, where she teaches a range of courses in literature, theory, and film, including a class on Stephenie Meyer in popular American culture. She has work published in national and international journals, and her first book, *Shakespeare in Transition*, was published in 2010.

Photo Credits